HOPSCOTCH
FAIRY TALES

Th...

Class No. _J 5-8_   Acc No. _C/237841_

Author: _WALTER A._   Loc: **6 – MAR 2009**

1 3 MAR 2012

...three weeks. It is to be
...st date stamped below.
...rged for every week or
...due

2 6 SEP 2012	1 1 MAY 2016	
2 6 OCT 2012	‑4 JUL סמבר	
‑7 AUG 2015		
1 6 OCT 2015		
2 3 OCT 2015		
1 1 DEC 2015		
‑8 JAN 2016		

First published in 2008 by
Franklin Watts
338 Euston Road
London
NW1 3BH

Franklin Watts Australia
Level 17/207 Kent Street
Sydney
NSW 2000

A CIP catalogue record for this book is available
from the British Library.

ISBN 978 0 7496 7899 9 (hbk)
ISBN 978 0 7496 7905 7 (pbk)

Series Editor: Melanie Palmer
Series Designer: Peter Scoulding
Series Advisor: Dr Barrie Wade

Printed in China

Franklin Watts is a division of
Hachette Children's Books,
an Hachette Livre UK company.

HOPSCOTCH FAIRY TALES

The Three Little Pigs

by Anne Walter and Daniel Postgate

W
FRANKLIN WATTS
LONDON•SYDNEY

Once upon a time, there
were three little pigs.

One day, their mother said, "You're old enough to build your own houses now. But beware of the big bad wolf!"

7

Soon the three little pigs
met a man carrying straw.
"Please may I have some straw?"
asked the first little pig.
"Yes," replied the man.

The first little pig quickly built
a house of straw.

Next, they met a man carrying sticks. "Please may I have some sticks?" asked the second little pig. "Of course," replied the man.

The second little pig quickly built a house of sticks.

Then the third little pig met a man carrying bricks. "Please may I have some bricks?" he asked. "Certainly," replied the man.

The third little pig worked all week long on his house of bricks.

The big bad wolf soon knocked
at the first little pig's door.
"Little pig, little pig, let me in!"
he called.

The first little pig remembered
what his mother had told him.
"Not by the hairs on my chinny
chin chin!" he replied.

"Then I'll huff and I'll puff and I'll blow your house in!" roared the wolf. He huffed and he puffed and he blew the straw house down.

The first little pig fled to his
brother's house.

The big bad wolf knocked at the second little pig's door. "Little pig, little pig, let me in!" he called.

"Not by the hairs on my chinny chin chin!" replied the second little pig, shaking.

"Then I'll huff and I'll puff and I'll blow your house in!" roared the wolf. He huffed and he puffed and he blew the stick house down.

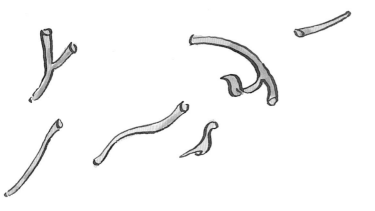

The two little pigs fled
to their brother's house.

The big bad wolf knocked at the
third little pig's door. "Little pig,
little pig, let me in!" he called.

"Not by the hairs on my chinny chin chin!" came the reply.

"Then I'll huff and I'll puff and I'll blow your house in!" roared the wolf again.

"Just you try it!" called the third
little pig, cheekily.

The wolf huffed and he puffed ...

and he huffed and he puffed ...

but he could not blow that brick
house down.

The wolf was very angry.
He decided to climb onto the
roof and down the chimney
to get his dinner.

Up he climbed ...

in he squeezed ...

and down he
dropped ...

29

… straight into the third little pig's cooking pot!

The wolf was never seen again!
The three little pigs celebrated
with a big party.

POP!

Hopscotch has been specially designed to fit the requirements of the Literacy Framework. It offers real books by top authors and illustrators for children developing their reading skills. There are 55 Hopscotch stories to choose from:

Marvin, the Blue Pig
ISBN 978 0 7496 4619 6

Plip and Plop
ISBN 978 0 7496 4620 2

The Queen's Dragon
ISBN 978 0 7496 4618 9

Flora McQuack
ISBN 978 0 7496 4621 9

Willie the Whale
ISBN 978 0 7496 4623 3

Naughty Nancy
ISBN 978 0 7496 4622 6

Run!
ISBN 978 0 7496 4705 6

The Playground Snake
ISBN 978 0 7496 4706 3

"Sausages!"
ISBN 978 0 7496 4707 0

Bear in Town
ISBN 978 0 7496 5875 5

Pippin's Big Jump
ISBN 978 0 7496 4710 0

Whose Birthday Is It?
ISBN 978 0 7496 4709 4

The Princess and the Frog
ISBN 978 0 7496 5129 9

Flynn Flies High
ISBN 978 0 7496 5130 5

Clever Cat
ISBN 978 0 7496 5131 2

Moo!
ISBN 978 0 7496 5332 3

Izzie's Idea
ISBN 978 0 7496 5334 7

Roly-poly Rice Ball
ISBN 978 0 7496 5333 0

I Can't Stand It!
ISBN 978 0 7496 5765 9

Cockerel's Big Egg
ISBN 978 0 7496 5767 3

How to Teach a Dragon Manners
ISBN 978 0 7496 5873 1

The Truth about those Billy Goats
ISBN 978 0 7496 5766 6

Marlowe's Mum and the Tree House
ISBN 978 0 7496 5874 8

The Truth about Hansel and Gretel
ISBN 978 0 7496 4708 7

The Best Den Ever
ISBN 978 0 7496 5876 2

ADVENTURE STORIES

Aladdin and the Lamp
ISBN 978 0 7496 6692 7

Blackbeard the Pirate
ISBN 978 0 7496 6690 3

George and the Dragon
ISBN 978 0 7496 6691 0

Jack the Giant-Killer
ISBN 978 0 7496 6693 4

TALES OF KING ARTHUR

1. The Sword in the Stone
ISBN 978 0 7496 6694 1

2. Arthur the King
ISBN 978 0 7496 6695 8

3. The Round Table
ISBN 978 0 7496 6697 2

4. Sir Lancelot and the Ice Castle
ISBN 978 0 7496 6698 9

TALES OF ROBIN HOOD

Robin and the Knight
ISBN 978 0 7496 6699 6

Robin and the Monk
ISBN 978 0 7496 6700 9

Robin and the Silver Arrow
ISBN 978 0 7496 6703 0

Robin and the Friar
ISBN 978 0 7496 6702 3

FAIRY TALES

The Emperor's New Clothes
ISBN 978 0 7496 7421 2

Cinderella
ISBN 978 0 7496 7417 5

Snow White
ISBN 978 0 7496 7418 2

Jack and the Beanstalk
ISBN 978 0 7496 7422 9

The Three Billy Goats Gruff
ISBN 978 0 7496 7420 5

The Pied Piper of Hamelin
ISBN 978 0 7496 7419 9

Goldilocks and the Three Bears
ISBN 978 0 7496 7897 5 *
ISBN 978 0 7496 7903 3

Hansel and Gretel
ISBN 978 0 7496 7898 2 *
ISBN 978 0 7496 7904 0

The Three Little Pigs
ISBN 978 0 7496 7899 9 *
ISBN 978 0 7496 7905 7

Rapunzel
ISBN 978 0 7496 7900 2 *
ISBN 978 0 7496 7906 4

Little Red Riding Hood
ISBN 978 0 7496 7901 9 *
ISBN 978 0 7496 7907 1

Rumpelstiltskin
ISBN 978 0 7496 7902 6*
ISBN 978 0 7496 7908 8

HISTORIES

Toby and the Great Fire of London
ISBN 978 0 7496 7410 6

Pocahontas the Peacemaker
ISBN 978 0 7496 7411 3

Grandma's Seaside Bloomers
ISBN 978 0 7496 7412 0

Hoorah for Mary Seacole
ISBN 978 0 7496 7413 7

Remember the 5th of November
ISBN 978 0 7496 7414 4

Tutankhamun and the Golden Chariot
ISBN 978 0 7496 7415 1

* hardback

/